KAALMANI

Aniruddh Reddy Ravula

ISBN 979-8-89519-528-4

Contents

Prologue

Kalanemi was an Asura King who was a great devotee of Lord Vishnu. He was having a special gem called Kaalmani. Using this he has the ability to deceive time and even magic completely. Lord Vishnu had been the one who had-despite all the gods *not* supporting his decision-given the Kaalmani to Kalanemi since he had been one of his greatest devotees. The gods had quickly realized that giving the Kaalmani to Kalanemi was quite an erroneous decision. Although, an exact limit to the Kaalmani's power was unknown-understandably,   considering that very few were even aware of its existence-it was a known fact that Kalanemi had been trying to find out how much power it possessed through his little 'experiments'. As Kalanemi began to wreak havoc upon the 3 worlds through his little 'experiments', the gods had found a likely opportunity to end Kalanemi's life in the Tarakamaya war, knowing quite well that Lord Vishnu wouldn't have any qualms over splitting the Kaalmani as not only would the cause be for justice, it would also ensure that the Kaalmani would be buried in history for a long, long time. Thus, During Tarakamaya war the Devas were winning the war, but to build confidence and morale in the Asuras Kalanemi used Kaalmani which showed that asuras are winning in the war.

The Devas had then sent a plea to Lord Vishnu to clear this confusion. However, Kalanemi hadn't been aware of how much power the Kaalmani contained and thus he had ended up with only being able to deceive time for a few hours.

Lord Vishnu then uses his Sudharshana chakra against Kaalmani. Due to the power of Sudharshana chakra Kaalmani got split into four parts and the 4 parts are distributed to various places. As it is hit by the noble Sudarshana chakra the four parts individually acquired good qualities like power of healing, power to control fire, power to control Tsunamis and to see that dharma is followed on the earth. But if at all the four parts are brought together by any evil force then Kaalmani will get its original quality of controlling time.

However, soon after the beginning of Kaliyuga, Lord Brahma asked Lord Maha Vishnu "Who will guard the four parts of Kaalmani in the 4th and final yuga the Kaliyuga" to this Lord Maha Vishnu replied in this way "O Pitamahah, O Swayambhu, when the Kaliyuga dawns each one of the parts will be with the solar dynasty (Suryavanshis), lunar dynasty (Chandravanshis), Markandeya Tirta and the fourth part will be under sea which controls earthquakes in the sea (Samudra Garba).

"O Adideva but the Kaliyuga shall make everyone develop negative feelings such as hatred, fear and jealousy, so how will the descendants of the Suryavanshis and Chandravanshis resist Kaliyuga...?", Lord Brahma asked.

"You will know soon enough O Chaturanana", Lord Maha Vishnu replied pleasantly.

Chapter-1

Unfolding Destiny

PADMAVATHI TEMPLE, TIRUPATI

Days of Navaratri

Nityananda kari, Varaa Abhaya karee,

Soundarya rathnaakaree,

Nirddhotahakila ghora pavaanakaree,

Prathyaksha Maheswaree,

Praaleyachala vamsa pavavakaree,

Kasi puraadheeswaree,

Bhikshaam dehi, krupaa valambana karee,

Mathaa Annapurneswaree

Ansh was singing the Annapurnashtakam in his melodious voice, it was as if the Annapurnnashtakam will only be good when it is sung by him. The priests and the devotees are mesmerized by his voice and immersed in the devotion of Devi Annapoorna.

Ansh is a day-to-day 17 years old teen, but unknown to him, his parents actually belonged to the famous solar dynasty, Ansh was quite tall for his age, well built and extremely fast, agile and quite quick in analysing his opponents and their moves. Ansh's paternal uncle, his father's elder brother Arjun had been secretly training Ansh in all forms of armed and unarmed combat since Ansh was six. Though Ansh didn't know it yet, his uncle was training him, to protect the part of the Kaalmani in their puja room.

Arjun is a well-known ayurvedic doctor and he acquired ayurveda through his parents and whatever the disease because of his hand and the way of his treatment, the disease will be treated. The fact which was unknown to everyone is that the first part of the Kaalmani which is in their pooja room has the power of healing. The healing powers are being transmitted through Arjun.

Once the prayer is completed Arjun had come to the temple to take him back to their home. Ansh's family was a joint family. Ansh was just about to enter his house, when the house suddenly burst into flames. Ansh shouted in shock, His parents, grandparents and aunt were in there! Ansh used his mobile and called the fire fighters, an ambulance and the police. Though all of them arrived, by the time they were taken to the hospital all were dead. Meanwhile his uncle went inside the fire to get the first part of the Kaalmani from pooja room, he gets it safely but he was injured severely with burns.

As his last words, he disclosed everything about Kaalmani and said that now it is Ansh's responsibility to protect the Kaalmani. His uncle also gave information about the Suryavanshis and Chandravanshis, and it should not go into the hands of dark forces who wanted to misuse its power and obliterate Bhulok 'the realm of earth' as well as Devalok 'the realm of the Devas'. He tells Ansh everything about all the parts of the Kaalmani and their locations and individual powers and about where to keep them safely when it was necessary, he said it was hidden in their own pooja room in a manuscript and asks him to get it before it gets burnt due to the fire. Ansh then manages to successfully get it out, miraculously without either, himself or the manuscript being injured in the very least. Arjun, who is on the verge of death extracts a promise from Ansh that he will protect the Kaalmani till his last breath and dies.

Ansh's first task is to protect the Kaalmani and it should not go into the hands of evil forces. For that he was looking for a safe place to hide it, Ansh identified a safe area near a temple in Sheshachalam hills and he kept it safely.

His second quest is to find the 2nd part of Kaalmani. Ansh knew that he has to locate the descendants of the Chandravanshis, and when he is about to exit the hills he meets a guru (Vyasa Maharishi in Disguise) who helps him in locating the second part of Kaalmani, by advising him to search in Vindhya ghats.

A FEW WEEKS LATER

In Vindhya ghats Ansh manages to track down the Chandravanshi descendants, but before he reaches there the 2nd part of Kaalmani has already been stolen by the seven bottom realms of Pataal. The dark forces and the creatures that had stolen the 2nd part of the Kaalmani had belonged to *Atala, Vitala, Sutala, Rasatala, Talatala, Mahatala and Paatala lokas* which were the seven bottom realms.

Now Suryavanshis and Chandravanshis together had a meeting and discussed about the danger that evil forces posed to Bhulok and Devalok and how to take the 2nd part of Kaalmani from them. They come to a single verdict that they all should fight against the bottom realms till their last breath.

In the Vindhya ghats they met two sages (Raja Mahabali and Kripacharya in disguise) who secretly train Ansh and other people in various skills which are important for warfare against the demons.

BATTLE IN UJJAINI (Solar and lunar dynasty versus 7 bottom realms)

Ansh, Suryavanshis and Chandravanshis were about to fight the creatures from the 7 bottom realms. He was curious and a bit afraid of what he might face, as he didn't know what kind of demon he would face. Ansh was still stunned that the modern-day world didn't know that Kshatriyas were living among them. Just as he had begun to ponder as to how the world would react to this, a conch was blown and the battle had begun.

7 DAYS LATER

Rain was pouring continuously upon them.

After 7 days of continuous war, sweat was dripping from the pores of all the Chandravanshis, Suryavanshis and Ansh who knew that they couldn't fight the demons much longer. Ansh's allies were fighting furiously but it was quite evident that, they would quickly lose the battle. Before Ansh could think of anything, Abhora appeared in a flash of light. In fact, when Ansh was fighting quite furiously with Abhora he said "O manava you are so weak and even more fragile, I thought descendants of the Suryavanshis were unbelievably skilled and powerful, but you are weak and helpless and you are a notable disappointment to your ancestors, if none of you can beat me than what hope do you have in fighting against Kaaldev?"

Turning towards the Chandravanshis, Abhora said 'I thought that all of you would turn out to be as mighty as your ancestors such as Arjuna, Bhimsen,

Dharmaraja even Duryodhana was a lethal war lord and a great warrior". Continuing Abhora said "Surely with great ancestors like this you should have been better than this". Abhora snorted in disgust.

Ansh was enraged and began lashing back at Abhora. Ansh moved a few steps back strategically, all of a sudden, he did a somersault in the air & tried a flying kick that might possibly stagger him, but Abhora didn't even flinch. Abhora sighed, *these Kaliyuga humans, they must have had quite the gall to even think that they could tackle the lord of Eternal Darkness.* 'Enough!' Roared Abhora angrier than ever. Abhora started fighting with Ansh furiously as well, but it was evident Ansh would lose the battle with a single miscalculation. Suddenly, Abhora then bent low, and Ansh seizing the opportunity that had presented itself to him took the 2nd part of the Kaalmani from him.

When 2nd part of Kaalmani was taken from Abhora's hands, a huge portal came out of the sky from within it arrived a horrendous being with 2 large horns a devilish face, dark and bloodied eyes. He had a muscular built with a glowing red armour and he had spiked clubs in his hands. He loudly yelled "I am Pralaya an amsh of Kaaldev.

"Master" shouted Abhora and rushed to kneel before his lord. Pralaya kicked Abhora saying "You fool! Our master hasn't completely awakened because you lost the part of the Kaalmani with you. As long as at least 3 of the 4 parts don't merge together Kaaldev can't fully get his evil powers to control Bhulok and Devlok.

"Not if I stop you first" said Ansh who came running towards Pralaya to fight with him. "I will take care of this insolent boy, my lord" said Abhora as he unsheathed his sword for battle. "No, I will have to test him to know if he can keep his emotions in check and if he poses any possible threat to me or our master's plans for the three worlds."

"But, my lord..." Abhora was rudely interrupted by Ansh who was suddenly lifted above the ground by Pralaya who seemingly possessed the ability of Telekinesis (The ability to lift physical objects or the physical bodies of living organisms, Telekinesis can kill or severely harm people and other organisms). Ansh was clearly struggling against Pralaya who might kill him if nobody rescued him.

Suddenly there appeared a white flash of light which seemed to appear from sky, it was seemingly in the shape of a cloud. From it emerged a man who looked lean but had a powerful figure. The man had black hair, a clear symbol of youth with

Rudraksha beads in his left hand and a tightly closed right fist.

He had a godly aura. He wore a dhoti and a simple cream coloured Angavastram. "Well, look what we have here" said Abhora in a ridiculing tone. "Rishi Markandeya, a pleasure to meet you" Pralaya then gestures to the 2 parts of Kaalmani and continues "I suppose you haven't come here to surrender your portion of the Kaalmani, have you?" Abhora was trying to ridicule and provoke the Rishi to attack him.

However, Rishi Markandeya was nonchalant. "No, I have come here for Ansh" said Rishi Markandeya pointing towards Ansh who became unconscious the moment Pralaya threw him down. "That's not going to happen anytime soon" said Pralaya calmly. "Then I guess I have to go the hard way" suddenly a gust of wind threw everybody except Pralaya and Abhora off their feet & then a mist of smoke appeared. Rishi Markandeya used this gap and teleported himself and Ansh somewhere safer.

Chapter-2

The Markandeya Tirta

Markandeya Tirta is a place where sage Markandeya worships Lord Shiva and Lord Maha Vishnu, which is present near Yamunotri in Uttarakand. Third part of Kaal mani is being worshipped by the sages and students of Markandeya in that ashram. This part of Kaalmani is meant to protect Dharma.

Sage Markandeya appeared in Markandeya Tirtha. Ansh is still unconscious but Rishi Markandeya was quite sure that he would recover in a day or two. Rishi Markandeya asked the Vaidya Raj Ashwini of the ashram, to look after Ansh. As he would play a vital role in successfully destroying Pralaya, Abhora and KaalDev.

Half of the ashram comprises of Suryavanshis and the other half comprises of Chandravanshis. There are a total of seven favourites of Guru Markandeya in the ashram, four of them being Chandravanshis and the other three were Suryavanshis.

The Suryavanshis are triplets namely, Amar, Anant and Ajay.

Amar is an expert at whiplash fighting, excellent hand-to-hand combatant and a very strategic & tactical person.

Anant could fire 4 arrows at a time, he is the best archer in the whole ashram which comprised of over 1000 students, he is also known as the "wielder of doom".

Ajay is an excellent mace-fighter, he is also very strong for his age. All three of them had jet black eyes a heavy build (though Ajay had the biggest build) and could run at superhuman speeds.

Then there are the Chandravanshis Maya, Guruva, Akarsh & Prithvi.

Maya knew light magic and how to use it according to her will, she could manipulate energy and dark matter, as if that wasn't enough, she is a very intelligent person.

Guruva has leadership qualities and he is an excellent spear fighter. He had done superhuman feats as a child, also he knew many mantras taught to him by Guru Markandeya which could trap powerful Asuras in a huge maze.

Akarsh is a maharishi who could use spirits to possess others to achieve superhuman feats for good. He can ask the spirits to spy on their opponents & tell him what they are planning.

Last, but not least Prithvi is blessed by Lord Shiva for her devotion at the age of six to possess superhuman strength, speed, intelligence & healing powers. All of them are adopted into the ashram at the age of five.

Two days later

"Aaaa! said Ansh, as he woke up with a start. The last thing he remembered was seeing a white flash of light before falling unconscious. He noticed that he is in some kind of temporary hospital before he could react somebody tried to push some kind of greenish substance into his mouth, before Ansh could try to struggle, he blacked out.

1 Day Later

Ansh woke up, pictures of what had happened started floating into his mind.

"Who are you people, why did you bring me here" asked Ansh in a daze. "We saved you from Pralaya and Abhora three days ago, so be grateful to us, said Akarsh. Without waiting for a response he continued "We are living near Markandeya tirtha under the able guidance and leadership of our Guru Markandeya."

"Listen to me, my son this might be a lot to take in for you, but let's go over it one by one" said Rishi Markandeya calmly. Ansh finally became peaceful & came out of his daze reassuring himself he was in the hands of the good guys. He then said "What do I do now?" "You need training" replied Rishi Markandeya.

A few days later....

The training given to Ansh by Rishi Markandeya was so intense that very few people could bear it. Ansh had to get up early in the morning and he has to learn telekinesis, telepathy, pyrokinesis, hydro kinesis & aero kinesis. He had to learn the Vedas, Puranas & continuous discussions & debates on the various topics of Dharma and understanding how to preserve Dharma in the world.

He was given training in martial arts and hand to hand combat and how to use weapons other than the sword. He listens to war plans, strategical discussions and learns military tactics. Along with war strategies he learnt how to mingle with different people to increase his communication skills. Every night before going to sleep he used to worship Trimurti, Tridevi & Ma Adishakti.

"I've been observing you since a lot of time Ansh, and I've realised you have a lot of potential in you, so I think it's time to join you into the group of Ashta Shakti Veers".

"Ashta Shakti Veers, what does that mean?" asked Ansh. "It comprises of 4 Suryavanshis and 4 Chandravanshis. It was predicted by Lord Brahma that when Kaaldev awakened and wanted to rule everyone in the three worlds eight powerful warriors of Dharma would stand up to destroy him, and their leader will be a devotee of Shri Mahavishnu with special powers."

"So, what does that have anything to do with me," said Ansh.

Rishi Markandeya said. "Ansh, you are one of the Ashta Shakti Veers to guard the Kaalmani.

Chapter-3

Meeting the Other Ashta Shakti Veers

"Am I dreaming" said Ansh in his mind. "Ansh, I know this is a lot to take in for you right now, but as the leader of the Ashta Shakti Veers you need to know everything about the rest of the Ashta Shakti Veers and you also need to meet them.

Ansh finally calmed down; he had learnt about many bizarre things in this world since past few months, he learnt that he was a descendant of Suryavanshis. His family is guarding a powerful artifact since many generations.

He finally spoke up "Suppose, just suppose I am an Ashta Shakti Veer, how do you think I can stop Kaaldev? after all, I barely fought against Abhora, & Pralaya who is only an amsh of Kaaldev and he would still have managed to kill me if you didn't appear on time."

"That was because you weren't ready to face Pralaya or even Abhora for that matter". "How do you think I can face them now" asked Ansh curiously.

Rishi Markandeya didn't respond instead all of a sudden, he threw a huge tree on Ansh using his yogic abilities, Ansh held the tree in the air, he had just done telekinesis! "Well, I can see that you're ready to meet the Ashta Shakti Veers."

In the practice ground of the ashram. "Maya, Guruva, Akarsh come over here".

"Yes, Guruji" all of them said obediently while racing towards him. "Where are the others" asked Rishi Markandeya. "Prithvi is worshipping Lord Shiva as usual, Amar is debating tactics of war with other students in our ashram, Anant is practicing archery and Ajay is eating food." said Maya.

"You all are Ashta Shakti Veers, I don't have a lot of time to explain why or how but this lad, called Ansh is destined to help you all to destroy Kaaldev. He also learnt all the skills required to fight with our enemies," said Rishi Markandeya.

By now Akarsh had called Prithvi, Amar, Anant & Ajay who were shell-shocked by the fact that they were the Ashta Shakti Veers who were destined to end Kaaldev." So, we have to hone our abilities in such a way that Abhora & Kaaldev himself can't defeat us" said Guruva.

"Yes, but for that you all need to understand your strengths & weaknesses so as to ensure that KaalDev can't exploit them to defeat your team".

"So, what should we do" asked Amar.

"You should all have to team up and attack me for this". "But, Guruji we are your pupils, we simply can't do this" argued Guruva. "We are only practicing Guruva because if you want to defeat demons like Kaaldev you need to first be able to defeat me, so just attack," said Rishi Markandeya.

"Alright guruji" said maya who instantly created a wooden barrier by cutting down trees as quickly as possible, using this she defended her team.

Meanwhile Ajay used his immense strength to throw the large boulders towards Rishi Markandeya, while Anant fired his arrows, Akarsh called for some of his spirit friends who started defending everyone by telling what Rishi Markandeya is trying to do, so that they would be prepared.

Guruva, Prithvi, Amar & Ansh were fighting with Rishi Markandeya from different directions however no matter how much they tried they were unable to defeat Rishi Markandeya. They tried for many days and failed badly.

One fine day, Ansh decided to call all of them for a group meeting on how to attack Rishi Markandeya. They made a plan which is as follows

1. **Maya** would use her light magic to temporarily try to trick Rishi Markandeya by making it look like there are multiple Ashta Shakti Veers who were attacking from multiple directions

2. **Anant** would try to fire arrows at Rishi Markandeya.

3. **Ajay** would rain punches on Guru Markandeya without stop.

4. **Prithvi** would distract Rishi Markandeya by running at an alarmingly high rate.

5. **Guruva** uses his spear to jump high in the air & launch many exploding fireballs on to Rishi Markandeya. He also chants various mantras using which he can disturb Rishi Markandeya, thus preventing him from attacking continuously.

6. **Ajay** will use his whiplash to attack and tie Rishi Markandeya's hands and chest to prevent him from fighting.

7. **Akarsh** will use telekinesis to push back Rishi Markandeya.

8. **Ansh** will use pyrokinesis, aerokinesis & hydrokinesis to continuously attack Rishi Markandeya and not give him a chance to defend himself.

All of them perfectly executed the plan and successfully defeated Guru Markandeya. "This was a test for your teamwork and all of you have shown your worth, Kaaldev hasn't fully awakened as of yet, however, Abhora & Pralaya the amsh of Kaaldev are hell bent on getting the Kaalmani and ensuring that Kaaldev rules the three worlds and that evil prevails over good. All of you have honed your skills to your best, so I'm sure that even if you face Kaaldev you can certainly defeat him."

The part of Kaalmani taken from Abhora should be kept at Gangotri which will be worshipped for manipulation of fire, and it should be kept in a secret place and should be fixed by mantras so that no one should dare to touch it.

Ansh along with the other Ashta Shakti Veers started moving to Gangotri and they hide the part of the Kaalmani taken from Abhora in the mountain range from where the Ganga River starts. They then perform a puja in such a way that it cannot be seen to a normal human being.

Chapter-4

The Battle Begins...

After fixing another part of the Kaalmani in the mountain range, the Ashta Shakti Veers come back to the ashram. Soon after, hordes of monsters started attacking the ashram, all the students started fighting with the monsters. Suddenly, Abhora came out and said in a loud voice "We don't desire violence, just give us the boy and the 2 parts of the Kaalmani present with you and we will spare your humble mortal lives".

"That will not happen," said Rishi Markandeya. The battle started by blowing a conch by Ansh. The battle seemed like an easy win for the ashram. Ansh went face-to-face with Abhora. "So, we meet again boy" said Abhora. Ansh used telekinesis to lift Abhora 6 feet up in the air and threw him hard on the ground because of which a lot of dust was raised into the air. Ansh had expected him to be injured and to call off the attack. However, after the dust and smoke settled Abhora came out unfazed.

Ansh is surprised by this turn of events. Ansh is like "How come...." unfortunately, before he could continue his sentence a glow emanated from him. He was again about to use telekinesis on Abhora, but he's suddenly distracted by this turn of events when Abhora who saw this as an opportunity to attack Ansh, was about to do so when Ajay who was nearby smashed the head of the asura who he was toying with & deflected Abhora's attack and bludgeoned his head giving Abhora an instant death.

"Keep your eyes on the battlefield" said Ajay sternly. Ansh nodded & said "I think I'm getting the energy from the Kaalmani. Once again, a glow emanated from Ansh, and he was back to the same point of time he was earlier.

Abhora shouted the retreat call for his army, realising that he has to inform Pralaya that they have to stop Ansh or else their defeat would be inevitable.

"The coward ran away," said Anant. "No, they needed to regroup because their army was not only divided but also crushed by our forces," said Amar. "Amar is right" said Guruva "Besides he might not have expected that our defence would be so strong".

"Which is why we need to be prepared for the next time they attack the ashram. And I realized that I'm actually getting energy from the Kaalmani and I'm reversing time itself" said Ansh who had finally accepted his destiny and he had also decided to take up the mantle of the leader of the Ashta Shakti Veers and to interact with his new teammates and learn their strengths, weaknesses and fears because that is what leaders do, they learn everything about their teammates/teams and use this knowledge to make weaknesses into strengths and after all knowledge is the most powerful weapon in the universe.

Chapter-5

The Final Crusade of Good versus Evil

Now Ansh is ready for a war against Kaaldev and his aim is to destroy Kaaldev completely. Otherwise again he might revive himself and try to join the four parts of Kaalmani to rule the three worlds. Ansh had interacted with all of his teammates and made especially strong & unbreakable bonds with Maya, Prithvi & Amar as well as Ajay.

Ansh did a pooja to the Kaalmani which is for dharma at Markandeya Tirta. Markandeya tirtha is like a piece of land on the mountain surrounded by deep valleys, and if anyone wants to attack the Tirta it will be visible to the people in the Tirta.

Guru Markandeya's spies witnessed some of the army of Abhora trying to sneak up on the northern border of the ashram. However, Amar & some of the other soldiers had warned that, they might have purposefully ensured they were caught on the radar so that, while the whole ashram was engrossed in defending the northern border, they could sneak from the eastern, western or Southern border and ambush them.

This was certainly possible as Abhora and his army were ruthless and would do anything to awaken Kaaldev. The ashram warriors got divided into four groups, Akarsh & Prithvi will lead the northern border with an army, the southern border was led by Guru Markandeya & Amar, and the eastern front was under the control of Anant & Ajay and last but not least the western front was led by Ansh, Guruva & Maya.

ON THE DAY OF SHIVARATRI....

While the rest of the country was celebrating the festival of Lord Shiva on a massive scale, the final battle had started. The battle between the asura army of Abhora and the ashram warriors started.

However, they had underestimated the power of Abhora who had realised that all the fronts were well fortified with powerful warriors to lead the armies in these fronts and asked Pralaya to destroy the northern front as it would down the other soldiers in the other fronts morally & would make it easier for them to defeat them.

Abhora prayed to Kaaldev for a lot of power so that he could get the location of the parts of the Kaalmani from Ansh and then retrieve them quickly. After getting a lot of power as a blessing from Kaaldev, Abhora flew towards Ansh. However, Maya stopped him. Abhora fought with Maya, Guruva and Ansh simultaneously, before them he was nothing by using divine Astras Ansh destroyed Abhora completely on the western front and they started moving towards the northern frontier.

Meanwhile on the northern frontier

Akarsh and Prithvi was busy fighting with Pralaya, after using divine Astras which were present with Pralaya in a much larger number than Akarsh or Prithvi, it was child's play for Pralaya to capture the northern frontier. After this news reached southern & eastern border the people are down in morale & self-esteem.

He attacked viciously and managed to absorb a Kaalmani part from Markandeya Tirta into himself by using strange mantras. Once Kaalmani reached Pralaya, Kaaldev awakened & returned from his eternal sleep.

Meanwhile Ansh, Maya and Guruva joined Northern frontier. After that Kaaldev said to Ansh "If anyone of you wants to stop me, you can't, because I am the eternal lord of darkness, if you truly believe that you can best me then you are a fool", then he continued "I don't care of the threat of the other Ashta Shakti Veers, but since you are a great warrior and a formidable foe, I suggest that you join me & let us rule the three worlds together"

"I can never side with forces as evil as you" replied Ansh boldly "We might not be able to stop you individually but when we are united, we can stop you" said Ansh and he & his team made a split-second plan hoping to defeat Kaaldev.

Guruva would chant some mantras using which Kaaldev would get trapped in a maze, afterwards he would start doing close combat with Kaaldev & whenever Kaaldev got the upper hand Guruva would simply be teleported by Maya to another place in the maze. Soon after Kaaldev gets fed up of playing hide-and-seek with the Ashta Shakti Veers & using all of his power destroys the maze.

Then all the Ashta Shakti Veers start fighting non-stop with Kaaldev, Guru Markandeya, Amar, Anant and Ajay also join the battle at northern front against Kaaldev.

Kaaldev realises that he has to divert them, if they worked together there is a chance that they would destroy him and he decided to divert their attention onto something else and he used a lot of his power in blasting Ajay. Suddenly they all stopped seeing that Ajay had fallen down. Out of his anger Ansh finally realized that the Ashta Shakti Veers might be having superhuman abilities and might be risking their lives to save the three worlds but in the end they too, were humans and that they too could die.

Ansh finally saw his inner self & his inner strength and prayed for Lord Vishnu to give strength and support to him in saving Kaalmani from Kaaldev and to destroy Kaaldev.

Ansh channelled the powers of the Asta Shakti Veers and using all of their power he made a white ball of shimmering light out of it and threw it towards Kaaldev.

That white ball hit Kaaldev's forehead which finally killed Kaaldev.

Simultaneously the Kaalmani with Kaaldev came in to the hands of Ansh. Once Kaaldev was destroyed, Pralaya the amsh of Kaaldev disappeared.

Ansh took the Kaalmani into the tirtha and by doing homa and pooja it was again fixed in the temple area. All the Asta Shakti Veers participated in the pooja and took the blessings from Rishi Markandeya. Ansh, knowing that he has nothing left for him outside of the ashram, he decides to stay back with his newfound family and lives out the rest of his days in peace.

Glossary

Introduction - Characters

Abhora - A powerful Asura, loyal to Kaaldev.

Annapurnashtakam - Sri Annapurna Ashtakam is written by Guru Adi Shankaracharya to praise and invoke the grace of Mother Goddess Annapurneswari.

Ashta Shakti Veers - The eight soldiers who are powerful and brave and fight for Dharma.

Astras - The Astras are supernatural weapons created by the Gods, and presided over by a specific Deity. In order to summon or use an Astra, one must have the required knowledge, i.e., the specific mantra that will arm, direct, and disarm the astra.

Chiranjeevis - The eight Chiranjeevis are great beings who are supposed to help Shri Mahavishnu's last Avatar Kalki in his battle against Kali. They are Ashwatthama, Raja Bali, Maharshi Ved Vyas, Lord Hanuman, Vibhishan, Kripacharya, Parashuram and Maharshi Markandeya.

Homa – A ritual performed in Hinduism.

Kaaldev – An Asura who always tries to control the Bhu-lok Patal-lok and Deva-lok.

Kalanemi – An Asura leader, he has fought against Lord Vishnu in Tarakamaya war.

Lord Brahma – The grandfather of all gods and demons, one of the Trimurti and also known as the creator of the universe.

Lord Vishnu – An extremely powerful god in Hindu mythology, one of the Trimurti.

Mahabharata – One of the 2 Hindu epics, the Mahabharata is a holy book comprised of 18 Parvas.

Navarathri – The Worshipping of nine goddesses during nine days.

Pooja – Worship of God.

Pooja room – A room where God is worshipped.

Pralaya – The Amsha of Kaaldev.

Rishi Markandeya – Sage Markandeya is one of the greatest saints of India. He is believed to be a great saint of both Saiva sect and the Vaishnava sect. He is one of the "Chiranjeevis".

Sudharshan chakra – The powerful weapon of Lord Vishnu which represented the flow of time.